MISSI

MISSING

by

Michael Edward Hammer

This book is independently published in the United States

missingnovella.com

Cover art: Hieronymus Bosch, "Ascent of the Blessed"
(from *Visions of the Hereafter* polyptych), ca. 1505-1515
Used under Creative Commons License

For MPH

Acknowledgements

I used to wonder why acknowledgement pages were always so long, even for very short books. Now I know. Even for a modest project such as this, there are so many people who must offer support, give of their time and resources, and provide their faith in order to make a work of art into reality.

The first time I shared any of *Missing* was with the amazing group of writers gathered together for a weekend at the Millay Colony for the Arts in the summer of 2017. I am so thankful for all of the help, inspiration, knowledge and kindness offered by those incredible people. Sofia Perez, Marilyn Bland, Courtney Reid, Marcia Blau, Caroline Crumpacker, and Naomi Huffman: thank you all so much.

For in-depth revisions of the first two chapters, I owe my sincere thanks to Dallas Hammer, Naomi Huffman, Rhonda Davis, and Casey Cobb. Thank you to all of the CRRL Porter Inklings for your positive reaction to Rob's chapter! For the final content edit of the entire manuscript, I give my most sincere thanks to Audrey Lockwood.

Making the decision to bring *Missing* out into the world felt like jumping head first into murky, unknown water. I was greeted by amazing support from so many, but especially from those brave souls who offered their support on Kickstarter; from Mary Maki, who gave me the guidance I needed on the publishing process; and Missy Egelsky, who has been a true believer and given substantive support at every turn.

I don't know if it's good for a writer to say that he can't find the words for something, but that's how I feel about my gratitude for all of you.

Stories

Reconnection

The sleigh bells on the café door jangled as James entered. He was gaunt, like someone starving, fed mostly by addiction, eating just enough to stay alive. Eyes hollow like a refugee or someone who had just survived a natural disaster. He might have been attractive once; he was tall; his hair was the kind of messy that some people paid a lot of money for. His now-dim eyes were still a catching shade of hazel. Those eyes darted around the room until he found her. He moved toward her quickly, desperately, like she was the meal he'd been waiting on.

He passed by the chrome-plated bar seats until he reached her booth. Route 66 and Elvis covered the walls; the Rock-Ola played the Beach Boys for some early morning pep. Just as he reached the booth, he stopped to watch her: her blonde hair fell in waves and her blue eyes were doubly bright on the cold, cloudy day. As she looked out the window, she was so beautiful. With one exception. Her eyes were bloodshot.

He stood for just a couple moments to burn her image into his mind. Finally, he sat across from her without a word. The woman didn't move or respond. He was glad. He loved the profile of her face.

James had always secretly had a thing for her. He hoped it was secret, anyway; he'd always been afraid that it wasn't. He could never express it because she had belonged to someone else – or maybe still belonged – even though her missing lover would never express his own feelings.

"It's good to see you," she finally whispered, turning toward him, smiling. It set his heart on fire.

James had always secretly resented being only her friend. He was, he believed, more attractive than her missing lover. He had a better sense of humor and was undoubtedly less prone to wild mood swings and grandiose madness. His own artistic vision was as powerful as anyone else's. His work was certainly more successful and well-received.

It was important that he never acknowledge the secret because the one she was with – or wanted to be with, anyway – had considered James one of his closest friends. And they were half-brothers, whatever that was worth. As much as he cared for her, James valued loyalty above all else. But he resented that, too – still, to this day. Being bound by a value to which no one else seemed to give a second thought. Bound to friendship even though he'd never asked to be anyone's friend. But this man – his half-brother -- had taken it upon himself to make James care, to be his friend, to take on all the burdens that friendship entails.

"Nykki, you could've texted anytime, you know that," he whispered back, hands still in his pea coat pockets. He shivered from the chill coming through the windows. Snow flaked down outside, finally. Despite all of the despair, perhaps this was his chance, finally, to show her that he was here for her.

"No, I couldn't. Everybody just reminded me of...everything."

He watched a lock of her hair – real blonde; Nordic blonde – fall over her forehead. How many times had he watched her swat that piece of hair back as she listened or laughed to her true love's voice. This time, he reached over and moved it back for her slowly. His heart raced as she looked up at him while he did it.

"Where have you been? What have you been doing?" he asked. In his heart, he felt he'd seen her yesterday, because he was always thinking of her. But in truth they had been out of each other's lives for two years.

She shrugged. "Working here and there. Surviving." The words had an edge he wasn't used to hearing from her.

He knew she wanted to talk. Her message had made that clear. But she was in no hurry, apparently, and obviously not interested in small talk. They sat in silence. The waitress dropped off a menu for him.

"I don't know how to bring up...the thing you texted," he said. His deep feelings for her and his confusion over her message made him uncomfortable and uncertain.

She nodded. "I understand. I hope you understand."

He forced an awkward half-smile and shrugged. "I understand *what* you wrote. I don't understand *why* you wrote it."

She was jarred; she sat upright. "What do you mean? I wrote it because he asked me to."

The waitress came back by the table. He ordered a coffee and some hashbrowns. He'd gotten up late and had to skip breakfast to meet her on time.

"He told you to meet me here so we can get everybody together back at the studio?"

She exhaled deeply. "I know it's hard to understand. I saw with my own eyes and I don't understand."

"When did he tell you this?"

"Right before I texted."

"Where did you see him?" His voice was harsh, like an attorney at a deposition.

"It...it's hard to explain."

He paused. He cared for her but silliness made him impatient. He'd never thought of her as a silly, simple woman, but he had learned in recent years to question everything.

"Try," he demanded.

"I saw... a man walking down the street. The man looked at me the way that he used to. It was like...he could see and feel everything that I knew about him. And he nodded his head, like he was telling me to come with him.

"That's it?" James asked.

"No. He said, 'Come on.' And I knew what he meant. He wanted to see us again at the studio. Everything made sense. He didn't look the same, but...it was him....

"*He didn't look the same, but it was him*?" James repeated the words, slowly, processing, in disbelief. "Why would he do this now? It's been two years."

"I know," she said, barely holding back more tears. "I know. Believe me," teeth gritted, forcing out the words with all her being. "But when he said 'come on,' I knew what he meant. He was telling me to meet him at the studio. And when I went and I saw him again in there, he didn't look the same – not the same as the man on the street -- but he was the same. It was like he knew everything about our place."

"You went by yourself to meet a stranger at an abandoned building?" James said.

She looked away for a single suspicious moment. "I went with Rob."

His face sank. "Of course."

She gave him a sympathetic look but said nothing.

James stared out at the sidewalk, suddenly feeling so distant from the normal world. Not that he had ever really known what *normal* meant, even if he'd wanted to know.

He could sympathize with her desperation. The grief and the guilt over what had happened had cost him the last two years of his life. The sleepless nights were filled with every moment, replayed on an infinite loop. What could he somehow have done differently? At least he had been able to

14

avoid homelessness by selling some of the paintings in the stash he had never wanted to sell; it was some of his favorite work. He hadn't been able to paint anything new in the last two years; his mind couldn't – still couldn't – move beyond the past.

This probably wasn't the time, he thought, to tell her of the wreck his life had been, too.

"You understand why this is difficult for me to accept, right?"

She nodded. "But you believe me, right?"

Suddenly, with heartbreaking clarity, he saw it. The weight of everything that had happened had overwhelmed her. He'd seen all of this before, the night they first met outside the club. She'd been living on the streets, raving horrific visions about her family -- some sort of trip gone bad – when they met her. Sitting there in the alley, screaming at the top of her lungs as they were about to go inside the club. The three of them – himself, his half-brother, and Rob -- helped her to the apartment they were borrowing. His half-brother insisted that they talk with her. The awkward looks of everyone watching them talk with this street person.

He saw it happen, and could still see the very moment she had fallen in love. All three of them had helped her, but her eyes locked with his half-brother's. He had carried her up the stairs. She never looked away while he was carrying her. James thought nothing of it that night, but then he rose the next morning and saw her sleeping on the couch, like an angel from a Renaissance painting, like someone had come by in the night to arrange her hair perfectly on the pillow. That was the moment he had fallen in love with her.

After that, every moment was excruciating. Every word she spoke was like honey; she was so wise and funny, it seemed to him then. Every time those words were directed to his half-brother, they became a sharp, stabbing pain. Every look she gave to his half-brother inflamed his anger.

One night James had heard her confessing to her love the years she spent under the influence of all kinds of demons. Out of her love for that man, she left all of that behind. Not that it happened overnight. It was a long, painful withdrawal and recovery. It was a miracle, just not all of a sudden. It was the kind of effect that he had on people.

James could not sleep for days after that. The senselessness of how she could not see that he could be there for her, too. But here they were again. His half-brother's protective force was gone. To hear all of this now was like being back in that alley on the first night they had met. Seven demons to take the place of one.

"Do you remember anything about the night we met?" He'd never asked her the question before.

There was no delay in her understanding his meaning. She bristled instantly. "I would never go back to that life. I would never do that to him."

"He's not here." He could feel the brutality in his own eyes.

She started to cry. "How can you say that? Is that how you really feel? Did you feel that way this whole time, this whole two years?"

The waitress arrived with his hashbrowns.

"Yes. Because he was reckless with his life and careless with the people he loved and he ripped my heart out." He had to pause for breath. "And I will never understand why you don't feel the same way."

These were, of course, lies -- he knew exactly why she didn't feel the same way -- but he'd learned to live with the cycle of anger that rotated with the unending guilt.

16

He wanted her to take the bait so badly. Go all the way down the rabbit hole, he thought. Get everything on the table. Fight every fight.

She had all the physical reactions of anger. A startled look. Flushed cheeks. But she took a deep breath. "Come with me and ask him yourself why he did what he did," she replied calmly. "After that, I'm going to get everyone together, to meet at the studio – the whole group, to meet him. Come with us."

"You're going to tell this to everybody?" Then, exhausted, he put his head in his hands. "Let's say, for one minute, that he told us to meet him. Let's just assume that, OK? What, exactly, am I supposed to ask him?"

"Ask him anything you want."

He only barely restrained himself from slamming his plate into the window. "OK. I'll ask him, hey, where have you been for two years? Why did you make us all care so much about you if you knew you were going to give up? Or how about, oh I don't know, *why did you kill yourself?*"

"He didn't kill himself!" she shouted. The waitress shot them a dirty look; a few uncomfortable patrons turned their heads.

"Well...I guess you and I just don't agree on the definition of suicide, then," James growled at a lower volume. "I guess I define it as putting yourself in harm's way, on purpose, so somebody else will do what you don't have the guts to do."

"If you think that's what happened, then you didn't understand him in the first place," she growled back, slamming her coffee mug on the table. "He was murdered." She spat the word at him. "He used his life and his art to stand up against all the things that everybody else just talks

17

about. And you know he didn't believe death was the end. He said that we live --"

He interrupted her with rolling eyes; he had heard the words so many times. "*We live forever through our art.* And I knew him a lot longer than you did," he tacked on for emphasis.

"Then why weren't you there when he died? Why was I the only one holding his hand when he bled out in the street?" He knew that she knew that she was stabbing him with her words. The strike came at a price; she barely choked out the last few words.

He couldn't take it anymore. "Listen to yourself! You watched him *die*. And now you're going to meet him this afternoon?"

"Is this how you really felt all along, that death was the end? Didn't we always say that our art came from eternity – that it was inspired by something greater than us? Isn't that what drove us to speak about something greater than ourselves?" She seemed like a different person, channeling these words of her lover's. He was caught off guard for a moment by her strength.

"It's one thing to believe all of that as a metaphor. It's another thing to believe that you are seeing a reincarnation – or whatever the hell this is – because some guy on the street looks at you."

"Why? Why is it so different, if we really believed it?"

He felt relief; this conversation saved him more years of caring about her. All the things he would have had to learn through painful experience were just revealed to him here. He felt as if a weight was lifted off of his mind. He threw a ten down on the table and stood.

She shook her head and barely kept from crying at his betrayal. "He'll be there. And I don't need to understand

18

why. I don't care why. All I know is that I would give anything to see him again."

James shook his head and paused one more time, waiting for his feelings for her to overcome the insane things she was saying. She was so beautiful, but these words unsettled him in his soul.

"Where are you going?" she asked. "Please don't go."

He shook his head. "I hope you get the help you need. But I've spent a lot of time trying to move on, and...this is just not it for me."

He raced toward the door. On this side of the door was a past he didn't want anymore. On the other side was normal. He was going to find it, to live it, to love it. Outside, in the normal world, he ran as fast as he could, toward whatever normal thing he could find.

The Pearl

Thomas' home studio was known by his students as a place of peaceful reflection and inspired creativity. He smiled, seeing these students rest now from their work, covered in paint, the three of them flopping down on the busted old cloth sofa in his den. He in turn sat back on the plush oversized chair he kept for himself; he watched them laugh and exclaim and wave their arms and tried to remember the memories of being that age that were finally becoming a little foggy. The impending crisis added a sharp pain to his bittersweet reflection.

The conflict had begun four semesters earlier. It had all started with trying to help the department cover for a sick colleague. The obligation seemed simple: four semesters, four sections per semester of Art History. Twenty years he had dodged it. His passion was in studio art; the teaching there was, quite literally, about creation. Art History was a totally different chore – an important course, but vulnerable to much more control from the bureaucrats.

--Can we help ourselves to the snacks, Professor?— the young Lana, like the other two a painter, asked so politely.

Of course you may but we're not in class so call me Thomas. It was all just teasing he knew and so he smiled; they always called him Thomas, even in class.

In his heart, he knew the truth: the crisis was his fault. It was his fault for agreeing to teach the courses. They were a drop in the bucket of all the teaching he'd done. What had happened was a series of displeased students and administrators. The course had been structured differently than his predecessor. The result, so They said, was material that was nowhere to be found in the requirements that the Bureaucrats had devised in their diabolical conjuring. He had never known anything about the so-called State Matrix that they had preached at him; it did not apply to the studio courses. The real problem had begun when They demanded changes to the course in the second semester.

And so it had begun. His letter to the student paper, published on the front page, denouncing the tyranny of the Bureaucrats. The dean's visit to his office that ended in the old man shouting at him. The accusations They shouted at him of angry parents and students though none ever appeared before him in the flesh.

What a mess. That was as far as his thinking could ever get on this dilemma. If not for the peace-giving chemicals working their beautiful way through his veins, he might actually have become angry about the situation.

Oh well.

Somebody was supposed to come by for an interview sometime soon about this vitriolic dilemma, from the school paper or something.

The students had asked to come over for an impromptu master class, to work at his well-equipped home studio. But they hadn't gotten very far before the marbled glass pipe was being passed around, and now here they were. His disciples lounged about, already feeling the effects of the quality sativa, relaxing on the couch in a tangled undergraduate mass of bodies.

Oh, youth. The beauty of it. The newness of each experience, such that one toke could give you a sublime trip for hours. Oh, youth. There is no substitute for you.

Thomas marveled at youth as its own form of art. Glowing skin: both the canvas and the paint.

How could art – art in all its forms – help but attract such beauty?

It seemed so natural that they would want to learn to paint and draw and sculpt; to bring to life all of the energy that flows through them. It seemed so natural to him that this was the reason that he had hungered to teach in the first place. It gave less time for his own work, but shaping and molding the energy of youth had been another source of vitality: the closest thing to the Fountain of Youth in this world.

More recent events weighed on the back of his mind despite the power of the dank bud. The institutional confines had begun to tip the balance; on one hand, the power of the creative spirit, and on the other, all the forces of bureaucracy working to tame and control that spirit. He had never understood why Those Who Have The Power would care more about dates and times and places – in forms and rules and structure -- than in nurturing this sweet gift of life in these young hearts.

How can they live with themselves?

Never think about how they snuff out the creative Life Force as it's just beginning?

Art is the realm of the abstract world.

Thomas pondered again the importance of every artist to emerge. Michelangelo mattered, of course; and Rothko and Klimt and Cezanne, and all those glorious others who had channeled Spirit into visible form. They each revealed some new idea about how the human experience could be expressed. By expressing it in a new way, they made it possible to experience **being** human in a new way. The peculiarities of place, the peccadillos of personality – those things washed away in the flow of **Time**. But together – together, these Artists were something more: the vessels of Spirit in the continuum of **Time**, joined together as sacred receptacles.

But the problem at hand was not Time as an abstract force but rather time as something to be memorized and written back down on a page by a student reduced to nothing more than a husk. He could not accept this requirement, and such was the nexus of the current situation.

Who really ever cared about memorizing the years that they created their masterpieces -- besides, that is, the dead-eyed Bureaucrats that wrote their curriculum rules in the state capital?

The question repeatedly burned through his mind. They tried to say – by implication, not by overt accusation, like in every authoritarian regime – that he didn't teach dates because he couldn't teach dates.

I'll write them a textbook just for the 20th century.

Just like the dead-eyed textbooks from the money vultures.

Fabriano 1423 Pala Strozzi Botticelli 1482ish Birth of Venus Caravaggio 1487 Bacchus da Vinci 1503 Mona Lisa Michelangelo 1504 David Rembrandt 1666 The Jewish Bride Eugene Delacroix 1863 Liberty Leading the People Picasso 1926 Artist and His Model Dali 1936 The Lobster Telephone and of course all the other things done through the twentieth century – there were Their sacred dates. That was what the Bureaucrats wanted the students to know.

But I see these students and I won't give in to pride because then I'd be just like Them.

Really it goes on and on -- there's probably somebody creating a new masterpiece right now which is the whole point but what does it matter They ask if I can't have them memorize and repeat all of this.

But now he was troubled by a question. *Had these students, so outwardly faithful in their learning, really wanted to hear more of his thoughts on the sublime nature of art? Or were they just using him?*

The boundaries of the question faded along with every other boundary in his mind, like a picture frame melting away and the picture itself expanding to fill all of the known space in the universe.

The desire for knowledge is as limited and finite as knowledge itself.

When we express our art, if it is from our souls, the divine itself is speaking through us.

Or at least can be. It can also be from the greedy part of the prefrontal cortex if we have the sick lust for money. Or from the genitals if we long to be pornographers.

But that is not SPIRIT -- be very clear -- SPIRIT AND FLESH are two completely different things.

He*, the Faithful One, the one killed by the City of Angels, the one killed for expressing the divine in a way that challenged Power, taught us these things before* **he** *went away.*

He *said when the artistic vision is pure the flesh burns away from the fire of Spirit. Man and woman become the same, even.*

I still remember how this idea felt like a fire in my spine the first time I heard it.

Oh how the bureaucrats would ruin me for **that**.

We can't have students touching the divine as part of their education.

Art takes us to the realm of pure Spirit.

Pure Spirit.

Pure.

Spirit.

The random thought of a time that I spoke this phrase in **his** *presence.* **His** *smile the hook that now grabs hold of my consciousness. Drawing to the place of gonedeadandburied rather than the place of Spirit still moving forward. The place of gonedeadandburied is a place of sighing and open wounds.*

Even tetrahydrocannabinol cannot always prevent the sadness of a memory.

I still feel the gaping hole in my heart.

At least I fill the hole with cannabis and not the delusion of **his** *reappearance.*

--Tell us something you haven't said in class before.— Tyrell said to him

Very well. Memorize and be true to this
mystery:

> *Spirit can become the paint on the canvas.*
> *Spirit is the canvas, painting.*
> *Sometimes Spirit is* only *the canvas.*

Each letter lingered on his tongue. S.

P.

I.

R.

I.

T.

He sang each of them for what felt like an eon. The sound waves echoed in his toes.

You should feel the divine like the Faithful One felt the divine when **he** *worked in every medium among us.*

He *was faithful to the artistic vision even to death.*

Is that where we all must go? Can we be faithful to the inner vision in life? Is that enough? Or is life so sufficatingly full of compromise that to touch the deepest truth means our inevitable demise?

How is that for something new?

Is that enough to jar you awake?

The chemicals we use to balance the mind are to help us wake up and find the Pearl -- not to doze off further into sleep.

Is this all I am to you?

Does the teacher talking justify your slumber? The teacher talks and so you think your job is to silently listen?

How empty it is to be a teacher, he thought. Perhaps people took the job only to fuel the ego, the chance to speak because some loved the sound of their own voices. Teaching is a form of arrogance, he believed, that somehow talking will change the world.

Did this paradox
drive him to his grave

?
What does this
mean?

Who asked?

The giant **bullfrog**

through whose eyes I'm looking?

Thomas carried on the secret lesson to his disciples:

*The Faithful One taught with words for sure but also without speaking through the openness of **his** heart*

*And the mastery of **his** craft*

Fully open to Spirit

Fully aware that Spirit would be sucked away before it could ever reach performance::hollowed out into something commercially appealing before the paint dried::

--Did you hear that someone painted a mural like the one **he** did?-- Erin asked

*It is only someone in touch with Spirit. It is not **him**. Spirit was in **him** but it was not **him**. It leaves us all in the tragic moment of life's final breath.*
*I know that Spirit dwelled in **him** even though **he** never said the thing that would have made Spirit within apparent:*

If man and woman take off their clothes and
trample them
seven times
under their feet
they would become the same and reach the divine

as though it were written in the glow of Haight and Ash at that glorious apex. How Spirit must have echoed through those streets before it was undone by the flesh.

Without Thomas realizing it, the reporter had arrived in the den. The young man sat patiently through the soliloquy, then interrupted when Thomas stopped for a breath:

++Can I ask you a question now?++

Where did you come from? Who are you?

Thomas was startled by the voice and face of this sudden ghostly appearance. He poked the apparition -- it was real -- in the flesh, at least.

++I'm here from the paper. To interview you.++

But you're only a child -- how old are you?

++I've been on the school paper for 3 years.++

How did you get into my office without me seeing you?

++It has two doors.++

No it doesn't -- there's only one door.

++There are two doors here -- I came through the door behind you, through the kitchen, the way you instructed.++

Kitchen? My office doesn't have a kitchen. What sort of demonic spirit are you?

++We're in your home.++

How did we get to my home?

The reporter had a bewildered look and offered no answer. Thomas was pleased; the apparition had no answer for that.

++So can I ask you a question now?++

You just did. Thomas refreshed his spirit with another taste of the pipe. A feminine arm reached out to him to grasp it once he was finished.

++So when did this conflict with the administration begin? About your art history class?++

When? When they decided that they were fit to judge where Spirit can and cannot flow. Because Bureaucrats turn not-importants into must dos. I turn must dos into won't dos. Ordering by date teaches nothing about freeing the spirit from the mundane deceits of the flesh.

The apparition scribbled some notes.

++How do you respond to the idea that the state is requiring knowledge that makes our graduates marketable?++
and something else Thomas refused to hear. Something about responsibility and such. *The same old statist horseshit*, he thought.

The most depraved thing I ever read was the idea that the state is the manifestation of the ethical ideal. Have you ever heard such a deranged thing? Most sentient non-savage beings with at least half a soul can see these words as patent shit. But yet we live in such a way as to accept the shackles of people who live by this idea -- and I use the word **live** *generously, which is to say breath and eat and work and repeat the cycle daily. Not the more true sense of* **reflection** *and* **choice**.

Does this answer your question?

Mumbling. Hemming and hawing.

He has no idea what I'm saying. Maybe the pipe would help.

The apparition declined.

++The president of the university has allegedly stated to the faculty senate that you are mentally unfit to teach due to the death of your friend, -----++

I know **his** *name. So what's your point?*

++The president has delivered to the Faculty Senate a letter stating that you are being investigated and that the rules of tenure do not apply because of the circumstances of your resistance.++

He'd known of that tyrant's demand for him to resign but not of the content of the letter. *Resistance? What does that mean?*

++Your refusal to implement state curriculum requirements.++

You mean by instead thinking and choosing and teaching about the creative essence?

++This course was Art History. What did you actually teach?++

Finally a decent question. We studied the only thing that really mattered: the creative process.

++How can students be properly measured on the "creative process"?++

They can understand and attempt to experience the various ways in which their artistic predecessors channeled Spirit into their work.

++So how can we have a school where success can't be measured?++

Where are you from? The school paper? The state propaganda machine, more like it. I feel the panic; inquisitors coming for me. It's OK. I'm in good company.

So many questions. It's making me hungry. How bound we are to the flesh.

You measure success based on whether or not students are more free than when they arrived.

++How do you measure freedom?++

Another great question.

The Bureaucrats measure in numbers. Freedom is measured through Spirit. The ability to express new and better ideas -- make new and better choices about life -- and new mastery of one's craft. Does this make any sense to you?

The apparition mumbled something about how he had everything he needed. The poisonous thoughts seemed to follow him out.

Conflicts like this and even the larger ones that take us to the gone places are all washed away in the flow of Life. In my weaker moments I will worry about the outcome but in my better moments like this I will feel Spirit connecting me to all other living things.

He smiled as the sweetness of slumber overtook him as it had already overtaken the others.

Rob

Rob had always hated how fat he was. Laying here in bed, on his back, he didn't have a damn thing to do but to watch that fat belly rise and fall with breath. He sat the bottle of whiskey on it, seeing if he could breathe slowly enough to keep it from falling over. Mission accomplished. He was quite well-practiced. Objectively, he knew he wasn't morbidly obese. When he was by himself, he would picture himself in plaid and cargo pants and an axe – as a woodsman, a Paul Bunyan with a nicely developed beer gut. He was a woodworker, after all. The look should've been a natural fit. But outside of his apartment, in the world, every pair of eyes he looked into, all he could think of was: fat.

He knew it was noon or a little after because the sunlight was shooting in from that one bent plastic blind that, of course, had to be right at the worst spot for when he was lying in bed. It was the worst time of the day. The morning's thoughts were still laying in shambles in his mind, but the sunlight said you had to start putting them together. There was at least some comfort in the routine. Up until now, in the morning, it was safe to just leave all that shit laying around. It didn't feel good to pick it all up and try to put it in order enough to get through the day.

The thought of going back to a therapist made his skin itch. The thought of group meetings made him nearly vomit. Talking to somebody was one of those things that wasn't even a conscious thought anymore; just part of the boiling pot of all the thoughts floating and stirring around. Pushing down, with any luck. You couldn't always make it happen. If things are gonna float, they're gonna float. But as long as you stayed in the routine, you could usually keep an anchor on them.

A knock. It was a soft knock, probably next door. But it was startling; it sounded close by. Nobody knocked around here. They laughed and yelled and sometimes fired gunshots and played loud music. But nobody knocked, and if they did, they'd damn well better holler through the door so you knew it wasn't the cops.

Wearing tank top and boxers – check. *Although I'd shoot somebody buck ass naked if I had to,* he thought with a smile. He grabbed his revolver from under his pillow and scooted quietly to the door until stumbling over the wicker ottoman. Slammed his belly and long beard against the door. Someone visible through the peephole. A woman. A gorgeous woman. Wavy blonde hair; bright, ocean-colored eyes.

Nykki. Looking straight ahead.

He jumped back from the door. Now sick to his stomach. He was dressed well enough to wave a pistol around in a tweaker's face, but not to see her.

He spun around, looking for pants.

Another knock.

"Hang on," he growled. And then tried it with a softer voice: "Hang on, one second," his voice a little higher pitch.

"OK." He heard barely through the door.

A pair of jeans hanging over his only chair. No dining table. Just an end table. The belt jangled as he fastened them. He jammed the gun back under the pillow and scooted back over to the door. He swung it open with his big, goofy smile and his arms outstretched to her.

"Hey, you!" he said, wrapping her up in his bear hug. She was tiny in his grasp; he lifted her to his eye level, and her feet hung about a foot off the floor.

"Hi, Rob," she said in a sing-song tone like a little sister would. He finally set her down and closed the door.

He saw her face again, and he saw a barely visible nose scrunch. Did he smell that bad? How many days since he'd taken the trash out? Rob thought that people assumed, because he was big and clumsy, that he couldn't see the little things.

Then he saw that she started to shake and her eyes turned red. Oh, god, he thought. What now? His ears rang; his heart rate spiked.

"What's wrong?" he asked.

She shook her head with a fake smile that came out crooked. He laughed. He always laughed in terrible situations. The more fucked up something was, the more he would laugh. To a point. And then the only way to cope was vigorous self-destruction.

"Come on. Nykki," he pleaded. "I haven't seen you in two years. I'd like to believe that you came over here 'cause you missed me, but…. What's wrong?"

She sat down on the bed – the unmade, unwashed for god-knew-how-long bedsheets – with clasped hands and a hard staredown with the floor.

"I saw *him*," she said.

Rob shrugged. "Who?"

"*Him.*"

There was no laughing now. Just a pounding racing heart. Tachycardia. The cholesterol and beer might finally kill me, he thought.

"I…I don't understand."

"I saw *him*. Walking down the street. I visited the studio – where it used to be, anyway – and then when I was walking away…*he* saw me. *He* smiled. *He* waved me in *his* direction."

"Did *he* say anything?" Rob asked in almost a whisper. He sat beside her on the bed.

She shook her head. "No. But I knew it was *him*. And…I could feel *him* say to me that we can see *him* again if we just go back to the studio."

Rob shrugged. "The studio's gone."

40

"The building is vacant again. It's for lease."

He knew what he should say, but it hurt so bad that he couldn't say it. He wouldn't say it.

There was silence. A slow, building silence leading to an inevitable climax. And probably a chaotic, destructive end. But Rob was determined not to break it. She would talk when she was ready. He would never be ready.

"What do you think?" she asked.

And then years' worth of tears bursting out all of a sudden – from nowhere except the dark, hateful places of his soul.

"I think if *he* was there I'd be the last person *he*'d ever want to see," Rob wretched.

Nykki put her arms around him and laid her head on his shoulder. "Don't say that! *He* loved you. You were a brother to *him*."

"Except when *he* needed me," the tears and the shaking wouldn't stop. Where was she years ago, before this guilt-cancer ate his soul – before it grew to a size that nothing could ever kill it now? Where were any of them, he thought.

She held him, rubbing her hand up and down his one shoulder, still laying her head on the other.

"You don't think I'm crazy?" she finally asked.

He shook his head. "I don't know what it all means. But no, I don't think you're crazy." He sniffled and wiped his nose.

Still a longer silence. Still huddling for warmth.

"Will you go to the studio with me?"

"Right now?"

He could feel her shaking her head on his shoulder. "No. Whenever you're ready."

"What are you going to say to *him*?" Rob growled quietly.

None of the things that might have mattered about her story really seemed to matter now. The experience of death and rebirth. Having a soul in another body – or what that even meant – especially to the person that might be carrying around that soul within their own soul. Or whatever immortality really meant. Somehow all of that was on the backburner while the years of unspoken thoughts were filling up the room.

Besides, whether *he* had returned or not, there was only one question Rob could ever ask. He'd played it on infinite loop in his mind for nearly two years. While laying down to sleep. The first thought waking. While brushing his teeth. While trying to cook and then throwing it in the trash and heading for the drive-through. *Will you forgive me.*

"I can't go back and say or do the things I wish I'd done," she said. Then sighed. "We can't ever be married now. I used to dream what it would be like to make love to *him*. I gave our children names. But...," another deep, then deeper breath, "I guess I have to learn to love *him* in spirit now. So I guess I would ask *him* why *he* came back for us. What we're supposed to do. How do we move on with our lives. How long can *he* stay with us."

Rob nodded. "That sounds like a pretty good list."

"What did the others say about this?"
"I came to you first. I knew *he* would want me to. I called John on the way over a few times but it just kept ringing each time."
"Thank you."
"Of course. I trust you. I don't trust easily."
She had never said anything like that in the past. He was surprised, but relieved. Rob thought he was the only one that questioned the group of artists that had been together at the studio.
"Who don't you trust?"
Eh. He would never get an answer to that question.
"Who *do* you trust?"
"You. John."
There had been a fairly large group at the studio, in its prime. He was surprised that the list of names was so small.
"What about James?"
She sighed. "No." And then with a bite of anger: "James was always jealous of *him*."
"Thomas?"
"Thomas is OK. He's always just so high and spaced out. I don't even know if he's there half the time."
Rob nodded. "That's true. Are you going to talk with anybody else about this?"

"Ya...I was going to call John again. I know he won't be too weirded out. And James, because I know *he* would want me to."

"You should try talking to Thomas. He's pretty open-minded," Rob said.

"Well...I was going to try to talk with everyone. But I was hoping you would go with me."

"To talk with everyone?"

"To see *him* first. And then to the others, so they'll know that it wasn't just me."

Rob took a deep breath. Now all of the questions – was this really real? – were ready for the spotlight. He rubbed his forehead. But above all, he cared about Nykki, and he'd always promised himself he would do anything to take care of her once she'd ended up alone again.

"Um..."

"It's OK. It's fine. You don't have to," she said, barely letting him finish the sound.

"No, no...I was just going to say, let me put on a fresh shirt." He slowly stood from the bed, grunting, lumbering into the tiny bathroom and hoping there really was a fresh shirt in there. A red tee shirt. Close enough. He stood looking in the bathroom mirror as he changed. The shirt wasn't too tight, thankfully; he could at least pretend he wasn't as fat as he was.

He kept trying to imagine what to expect. He wasn't nervous, really, because it was hard to imagine really seeing *him*. But imagining, what if, just in case – what would the conversation be?

Can I really handle it if he's *angry with me? If it's* not *real?* He asked himself this over and over while looking in the mirror, leaning forward, hands on the sink rim.

"You doing OK in there?" she called.

He snapped out of it. "Ya. Ya, I'm coming."

He followed her out of the apartment, opened the door of the pickup and helped her up. He grinded the old stick shift – an old floor shift – into gear, the transmission whining when they started out.

The palm trees danced in a light breeze. He pulled onto the main road and put his sunglasses on. It was bright out that day on this surprisingly pleasant winter's day. Or maybe he was like one of those fishes, where their eyes eventually just go away because they live in the dark so long.

"So, uh, have you been doing any woodworking?" she asked, awkward, stuttering.

He laughed. "It's OK, Nykki. We're both thinking about the same thing."

She laughed too. "OK. Because I'm sick to my stomach right now. I'm so nervous."

He nodded. They said nothing.

The studio wasn't in a great part of town, but it was a step or two up from where he lived. It was old, but not dangerous. Mid-century townhomes with toys in the frontyard, a sign of the young families moving in. The sights and sounds of the warm afternoon were in full bloom. Warm, dry breeze. Sunlight that turned the horizon yellow. The low hum of the wheels. The smell of exhaust and warm rubber from the endless lines of traffic.

Nothing but silence in the cab of the truck.

He parked in front of a white brick building, large windows, on the corner accessible from two streets. Deep breath. Heart pounding.

"Are you OK?" she asked him quietly. "Are you sure you can do this?"

His heart kept racing. He wasn't sure.

"Let's go," he choked out.

They climbed out of the truck. The walk to the door seemed like an eternity. He pulled the old key out of his pocket; he was a little surprised when it still worked.

To anyone else, it would be like nothing had ever happened in there. Concrete floors and a couple white sheets still hanging from when they had divided equipment into different parts of the studio. Stale air, dank smell. He could hear the ghosts of the past, but he knew they were only in his own mind. Air hanging thick.

The space was once cluttered. It buzzed, full of energy, the inspired students and the group of artists, coming together to open the place. Full of the hope that their work would change the world. Easels, lathes and kilns made it seem that the space was going to burst at the seams. Now it was wide open, stretching out over all 10,000 square feet, even though it seemed like more.

"Did he give you a time? Or a day?"

"No," she answered.

She understood the deeper implied question. "It just felt...immediate. Like I should be here."

"It's OK," he said. He paced around, hands in pockets. Empty spaces and stains on the floor made him turn his head away.

"I brought something," she said. From her purse she pulled a wreath made of silk flowers. The flowers ringed a picture of her with her missing lover. She sat it against the metal beam adjacent to the door.

"That's nice," he said, forcing a smile.

She clasped her hands and looked solemnly at the memorial.

Footsteps, from where they knew the back entrance to be. Leather heels clacking in steady rhythm on the concrete.

Tall. White. Black suit and tie. Like he should have a martini in his hand.

"Is that the guy you saw?" Rob whispered.

She shook her head.

The landlord, he thought. He pressed his hand gently into her back to motion her toward the door.

"We're sorry, we're just leaving," Rob called to the man.

"No need," he said. "I'm just examining the space." His diction was even and precise. None of the warmth that *he* had had.

"So are we. But we're done," Rob said, beginning to feel anxious, waving her toward the door.

"It's *him*," she whispered.

"You said it wasn't," Rob frantically whispered back.

"It's not the one from earlier – but it's *him*."

It did not feel like *him*. No spirit discernible in that capitalist wrapping.

"What do you want?" she asked the man.

He paced the room at a distance. "This is a nice space. There used to be an art studio here."

"We know," Rob said, curtly.

"Is that what you want? To start the studio again?" Her voice sounded almost desperate.

The man was still looking around the room, never at them. "I like for spaces to find their purpose."

These words stung Rob. *He* had said something like that years ago. About the empty spaces in two dimensions. The choice of where not to draw or paint.

Silence.

Finally, the man looked at them. The man's eyes felt like a sharp stab in Rob's forehead. His single look dredged memories he hadn't considered in years, versions of himself that had never lived. The banker that his father wanted him to be. A Sunday grill-out with the family he'd never had.

"This space isn't mine. It needs you two."

He turned and walked back out from where he had come.

"Wait!" she called. She ran toward the back exit, behind one of the curtains. Rob followed, worried at what she might do. But there was no need. She hadn't followed the man. He was already gone, and she was there, kneeling on the floor, crying into her hands.

Rob knelt down, slowly, his knees already getting stiff early in middle age. He put his burly arms around her. He sat with her until she started to breathe a little more normally.

"Come on. Let's go," he said.

The drive home was a lot like the drive there. Silence, fidgeting. But, in his mind, the heaviness hanging over her had the density of a blackhole.

"You OK?" he asked.

He could hear her fingers gliding across her cheek and a quiet sniffle. "Yes."

"At least we saw *him*," he said. His voice was as cheery as possible.

"Do you think so?"

A long silence. He cleared his throat. "Yes."

"*He*'s right. We need that space. We need to bring everyone back together, to go back to the work that we had started."

Rob looked at her sideways from behind his sunglasses. "I think you were right. We should talk with John. Then we talk with everybody else."

She wiped her cheeks again. "I guess that's why I was so upset. *He* didn't say anything else. I didn't feel anything else. What if no one else sees *him*?"

"If this is real, we won't be the only ones. *He* won't leave us abandoned." *Not again*, he thought.

"I didn't feel it, that urgency, or where to meet *him* next."

Rob shrugged. "Maybe getting everyone back together is really the thing to do. Maybe we'll feel *him* together."

"That's a beautiful thought."

She smiled, first at him, and then out the passenger window. He was unsettled; his stomach ached; he literally felt like he was starting to spin. He needed a reason to pull over the truck.

"Let me show you something." His words pierced the perfect silence.

They passed through another light then turned right onto the next side street.

"Where are we going?"

He did not answer. Nonetheless, the path they travelled was familiar to them both. It was the road that wound around to the place where they used to gather for drinks or coffee after a long day at the studio. It was also the place where the terrible night happened. Rob pulled into the alley behind the shop.

"Oh my god," she cried, covering her mouth with her hands.

"Do you like it?" he asked quietly.

On the back wall, on the alley side of the shop, was a mural painted in a blend of base and psychedelic colors. It was like something pulled violently out of Picasso's brain and left underground to ferment like kimchi – a fractured distortion of violence and screams and the heavens ripping open to weep. But there was no mistake: anyone who was out in the neighborhood that night – and there were many – would know what it really was. If anyone needed any recollection, it would be easy: *his* mural, the one he had worked on that night, was on the adjacent wall facing the side street. *His* mural was unfinished, now beginning to fade, but easier to see along a main road.

"Where did it come from?" she asked, determined not to cry in front of him again.

"I started on it about a year ago. I could only do it a little bit at a time." Rob cleared his throat and looked away for a minute. The truck engine kept rumbling as they idled.

"It's incredible. I didn't even know you painted."

Rob nodded. "Ya, I have two degrees. Painting and 3D. It was just easier to make money doing woodworking, so...that's the way I went."

She kept shaking her head, almost involuntarily. "It's almost like *he* painted it. I mean...you just captured *his* style so well."

"I tried. I felt sometimes like *he* was helping me. It never felt like a struggle."

Nykki slid across the bench seat and hugged him again. "It's wonderful. I'm so thankful for you."

He stroked her shoulder. "I'm thankful for you, too."

"Let's go talk to John," she said, determined again. "And then I'll call James. It's time to make the studio live again."

The Celebrity

"We're going live in two," the set director called. The studio ran like a well-oiled machine; it was only fitting for the top late-night show on cable news. In the center stage sat two middle-aged men. One was white with curly, greying hair and rough skin covered up by expert makeup work. The other had the distinguished look of a guru or diplomat; he was bald, his skin an olive-tinged shade of tan. His horn-rimmed glasses perfectly complemented his trimmed white goatee.

Piers Longmont, the anchor, the budding British celebrity on this American channel, nodded brusquely to his guest. "Ready?" Just another day at the office, the tone of his voice said.

Piers' guest nodded with an equal level of detached condescension. The man, in his blue seersucker and a blood red cravat, would clearly not be intimidated by such a trifling occasion as this. Some sort of electric brew boiled behind his hard, dark eyes.

"And live!"

Longmont smiled directly into Camera 2. "And welcome back. We're here with our next guest, Paul Gabashvili, author of the provocative new book, *The Teacher Within*. Welcome."

"Thank you," Gabashvili replied with a perfect smile and perfectly measured tone.

"Could you explain to our viewers the message of this book, and why it has rocketed to the top of the book sale charts before your book tour has even really begun?"

"The book speaks to a universal desire to discover our 'true' selves by, paradoxically, connecting to something greater than ourselves. The book shows readers the steps of how to channel and build that reality by drawing from my own vision, a vision that opened me to that connection."

Piers was not visibly moved by such esoteric statements. As though he may not even have been listening, his eyes flitted to the prep sheet and back to his guest.

"This vision that you describe at times in the book has certainly been the most widely covered part of your work so far. Surely this is because the vision involves an appearance – a mystical appearance, you call it in the book – of an artist who was killed right here in Los Angeles in a very highly-publicized event."

The author nodded; beyond this, he remained silent. Piers was caught off guard. This was normally the place where guests would speak for a solid few minutes on their own. The host nervously stuttered and looked for his next questions. The crew shot looks to each other. Nonetheless, Piers shook his head and carried on.

"Interestingly, you never discuss the exact nature of your experience or vision – however you prefer to call it – in the book. There has certainly been a great deal of speculation on this issue on social media. Do you plan to describe your experience at some point more in the future?"

The author shrugged. "If there were to be some need, I suppose I could. But I don't think more detail means that the experience is more valid. What happened and was said was for me; it may be different for others who have experiences of their own."

Longmont had developed his reputation because of his willingness to push guests with repeated, sometimes aggressive, questions. It was clear to the crew that tonight would be no different.

"There have been those who say that the lack of detail means that the experience in question has been fabricated.

How would you respond to those who say that the story of this vision, the lack of details, is just a way of selling books?"

"I would point to the fact that the book is an international bestseller. If that many people have been touched by my message, I'm really not that concerned about the critics."

Finally, Piers sensed that there was blood in the water. He always longed to find the moment of dominance in these interviews.

"Well – how would you respond to those who say your book sales are just proof that your experience has been sensationalized?" He flashed his trademark head-wagging smile at Camera 1. It was, in every broadcast, the visual representation of his moment of triumph.

"I would say that beyond the sales are the stories of those whose lives have been changed."

Now finding himself frustrated in his effort to seize his prey on this issue, Piers nodded, moving along briskly, dutifully, through his list of questions.

"Since the book was published, there have been interviews with some who knew the artist in question. There has been some controversy because these individuals also claim to have seen some type of appearance – appearances they describe very differently – of the same artist that you claim to have seen. These same persons also say that the artist who came to you in this experience of yours was someone you never met while he was alive. How do you respond to this?"

Gabashvili smiled. "There are several issues there, Piers. Firstly, to say that I never knew him when he was alive – I would say that he is alive now, which became very clear to me when he first appeared to me. So when you say *alive*, I think what you mean is when he was alive in his previous form."

Piers just barely avoided rolling his eyes. "OK."

"So if we look at immortality in this way, as a transition between forms, then none of these questions really matter. My experience will be different from others' experiences. But they both involve being touched by this man – this being – in a way that changes our lives."

Piers again nodded almost absentmindedly. "Some have said, though, that this is merely opportunism available because of a high-profile event."

Gabashvili shook his head very slowly. "That is a baseless accusation. I share what has been revealed to me. If you examine what I say, you will find that it is no different in any material way than any other description of this event."

Piers moved along and the interview wrapped in what seemed like only a few brisk moments. The two men smiled and shook hands at the end.

"I think your sales are going to continue to do well," Piers said.

Gabashvili returned the pleasantries and headed for the exit of the studio without any further delay. He was met by his personal assistant, Katie, and press relations strategist, Tara, who worked in-house for the publisher. Both had the typical look of ambitious young professionals – eager and haggard, fatigue held at bay by enormous volumes of caffeine. Yet both had traveled with him on his previous book tours, so they understood exactly what they were in for. They both glowed and smiled at their employer.

"Fantastic job," Katie said.

Tara, a little older, a little more detached, still nodded. "Yes, very good job. He's a tough interviewer."

Gabashvili smiled. "Everything is possible by faith."

Katie looked down at her phone. "This is our last obligation tonight. Can I get anything organized for you?

"Has there been any response to our requests to speak to Ms. Lamont or Mr. Kolbach?"

Katie shook her head.

Tara put her phone away and shrugged. "I think you've handled the issue just fine. If you can handle it with Longmont, you can handle it with anybody."

"It's not about handling issues," Gabashvili said. "Being here in the city is a unique opportunity to connect our movement with theirs. Explore the possibility of connecting with James Kavanaugh."

"Who?" Katie asked.

"The artist's half-brother. Different last name, but they did grow up together."

Katie nodded dutifully. "We haven't talked about dinner arrangements." She seemed to be barely awake, but she would not be found derelict in any detail of her responsibilities.

Her boss smiled and patted her on the shoulder. "It's OK. You two have had a long week. Take a break tonight. We'll meet at the hotel café in the morning."

"At our normal 8 o'clock time?" Katie asked.

Gabashvili nodded. "Have a good evening."

The two departed and he headed for the rental Lexus. He would be in the city for nearly three full days. Anytime he would be in a place for more than a day, Katie knew to procure for him a rental car.

He started to turn the ignition but didn't. Something changed suddenly in his posture and disposition. Rain started to pour down. He sat with his hands on the wheel, fighting back tears in his eyes. It was the worst feeling to him – the post-adrenaline lull. The act of performance

55

cleared the mind. As the tide receded, the underlying structure of thought and emotion could reemerge. Thoughts in this place were always so much more fractured than the man he was on the television screen, a fact of constant frustration to him.

He pulled out his wallet and looked at the picture, a woman and a small girl. The totem that must be constantly held. It could keep him grounded as his legs felt numb or when the world started to spin. Still he felt the tell-tale signs, the sweaty palms, the fast breathing. He was in no condition to drive.

He managed to slowly escape the parking garage and park the car on the street before his hands began to shake. He saw some sort of bar or coffeeshop across the street, about a block and a half away. His eyes fixed on the lights inside. People were lifting cups to their mouths, carrying on in a normal sort of way. He pushed the driver's door open, slowly lifted himself out of the driver's seat. Like a drunk man he staggered and swerved across the street and down the sidewalk. The rain felt like it sizzled on his hot skin.

He pushed the café door open tentatively, looking around the room several times. There were only a few customers, but the establishment was very high end. An offering of fair trade coffees and top shelf liquor. He ordered his evening green tea. The news network played on a couple overhead televisions. The bartender pointed up while he fished out a teabag with the other hand.

"Hey, you were just on TV. Cool looking book, man."

"Thank you."

A couple of the slumped-over forms at the bar looked over to see what unknown celebrity was causing all the excitement.

Gabashvili sat at one of the small tables by the window. He looked out on the now-pouring rain as he sipped the warm drink. The bartender delivered the tea in its own small metal pot; a teacup and saucer, sliced lemons and a tiny carafe of milk rounded out the service setting.

He did not notice the man a couple tables over before he began to speak. "I just saw your interview." He was a hipster looking fellow, still looking up from his laptop and taking out the strange wireless earbuds even as he was speaking.

Gabashvili couldn't read the young man's tone; it wasn't exactly a compliment, it seemed. "I'm glad."

The man pointed to his device. "So what's the deal? Did you really talk to a dead guy?"

The question he'd heard at least a thousand times. Always the same answer. "I saw what I needed to see."

"That's the same bullshit you said already. So what's the truth?"

He was certain now that this wasn't a friendly conversation. What was the meaning of it, the potential pros and cons now of further engaging? In this age of social media, the man could be livestreaming every word of this conversation. Gabashvili thought carefully about his response as he steeped the teabag and carefully wrapped it around the silver teaspoon. He was not resentful of the young man's anger. He understood it well, and it gave him the chance again, almost unconsciously, to be the man he wanted to be – the man that this same fellow had just seen on the television.

"The truth? The truth is that death is a cold, unforgiving reality. The visions that we call spiritual visions are the reassurance that death is more than a random, pointless force. They give us the conviction that life carries on in many forms no matter what we've lost." He had never found these exact words before. It felt, in that moment, like another voice guiding him.

"That's not my experience," the young man said, suddenly with a more quiet voice.

"How so?"

The young man shrugged. Belligerent energy manifested in refusing eye contact and shuffling scraps of paper around his table.

"Tell me about it," Gabashvili said as quietly and gently as he could.

"When I lost my brother, there wasn't anybody showing up to tell me how it was okay. My brother didn't show up and start talking to me the next day after we put him in the ground. We're just hairless apes on an insignificant planet spending a little time before we die." Tears fueled the almost-shouting voice.

"That's not what you want to believe, is it?"

"Well I don't want to believe in gravity either, but it is what it is."

"Gravity isn't the same as life. Life is its own force, a mystery that we don't understand in any meaningful way. I've felt that same loss as you, my friend, and I consider myself fortunate that there was something there to pull me back from that abyss you feel. There are those who can speak to that experience even when you don't have it yourself."

The young man finished packing his device and papers. "Well, I'm happy for you. Maybe I'll get lucky one day." He left quickly with a sarcastic wave.

Gabashvili returned his gaze to the window and the pouring rain. It was no lie – he knew exactly what the young man felt. What he felt now, the adrenaline pumping through his veins, was sufficient to pull him out of it; to connect him to a deeper purpose. It was the reason no one would ever know why he was so protective of that moment that connected him to the world of the living again. He would never subject that precious gift to the scrutiny of angry, doubtful minds, to be passed around as a meme on the endless, deranged circus wheel of social media. In this vindication, he peacefully finished his tea with a smile.

Reunion

The woman from the TV station couldn't stand in one place. Elizabeth Menendez, the most well-known field reporter in the city, was the best person they could have asked for to promote the event. But she was making Rob nervous; Nykki worried that she would trigger the PTSD that he worked so hard to manage. Menendez flittered around without end, giving the most minute direction to the cameraman and boom operator as they prepared to go live.

James was focused on Menendez's every move. He watched her like a predator on the Serengeti, waiting for the moment to pounce on his prey. Or maybe he was just interested in protecting himself from what he sensed was some other predator. Nykki couldn't really tell which. All she could tell for sure was that, even by James' pretty low standards of sociability, he was on edge and bitchy. She smiled at the thought of calling him *bitchy*.

But really, she was worried about Rob and about the newcomer. Rob was already a nervous wreck about this whole thing. He normally went out of his way to avoid cameras and events with crowds. When she'd first met him, he'd been doing woodworking professionally for a few years. He had told her later that his therapist had recommended visual art as a self-calming mechanism, a way of handling whatever was going around in his mind when he'd first come back from Iraq. What began as art therapy eventually became his career. But even then, years after he'd started, she could see in his eyes right away that he had seen awful things. He kept to himself and was pathologically shy. It took months for her to sneak up on him quietly enough to be able to see him work. One day they had finally talked after he'd finished working on a beautiful statue that now sat in front of city hall. He was still so skittish even after he had seen her on the worst night of her life.

Rob had been under more and more stress throughout this whole process. First there had been the meeting with everyone from the old group who would come or who they could get in touch with. He had stood there and supported her as they had talked about how the studio should be opened again – and why. John was willing to help. Thomas never showed up. James also refused at first.

When they had met together as a group that first time there were several others who said they'd had an experience like hers. Junior talked about how he'd had an unsettling conversation with a man who seemed to know everything about his art. Marr and Zack described a long conversation with an old veteran in a wheelchair who disappeared all of a sudden.

Then there was the moment that cemented their bond. As they met and discussed all of these experiences, a man who looked to be the twin of their lost friend came through the door of the library meeting room. He said nothing and in a moment he was gone. It was not the largest meeting room but it was large enough that someone could stand in the back without notice. Nobody remembered afterward who first saw the man, but many of those who were there swore that they saw him. But some did not believe it had happened.

So they planned to go it alone, her and Rob and John, along with some of the original group who had been moved by these experiences. She enjoyed those early days, cleaning up the studio, going to auctions to buy or trade for enough equipment to get started.

But then James finally decided to get involved. He never shared with them exactly why he had changed his mind. He said simply that he had had a vision.

It was just his way to be so overbearing. Projects that had already been underway suddenly had to be done his way. Equipment had to be re-arranged, or it wasn't good enough. Anything he could do to mark his territory. He was a natural foreman, a born company man.

And then the newcomer. Paul Gabashvili. They all knew the name. He was more well known for their story than any of them. James first introduced the stranger to the group; Paul said he heard what was going on with the new studio and that he wanted to help. He just wanted to be in the background and help the cause, he said. Nykki had never known anyone less capable of being in the background. He had rearranged his book tour in order to stay in Los Angeles longer and help prepare the studio. But he showed up to his first workday in a white suit and black shoes – the same get-up he was wearing today – and then they had two foremen.

John was the first to have enough. John didn't have Rob's inner demons. His emotional blank slate meant that he could turn the energy not spent wrestling with those inner things toward his art instead. He was a decade younger than the others, too; he was full of energy and rarely saw a reason not to speak his mind. So he told James and Gabashvili that they were out of line; it wasn't their place to come in and lord it over everyone else. John was heading east and was going to carry on his work there. At least that's the last he'd told Nykki. After the blow up, none of them had heard from him again.

Not too long after that, Marr and Zack enrolled at the university and said they'd be studying with Thomas instead of at the studio. But through it all, mostly on the back of

Rob's work and his mild diplomacy between the two foremen, the studio was finished. It was a beautiful feeling on the day when everything was finally cleaned and ready to open. And more than being just a place to do art, it was also a place now where they would reach out with art to those who were less fortunate. They'd worked to set up after-school programs and even some on-site activities for young kids. They worked with other artists' groups to set up an annual memorial event to remember the fallen friend who had inspired all of this.

To his credit, Gabashvili had arranged a lot of these things. He was the only one who had the connections to get a major TV station on the scene to report on their opening day. And even when he didn't know someone, he was the one with the personality and wealth to get in the door and make something happen.

So he had earned the right to be here on this day, in her view. But none of this was able to make Nykki ignore the feeling that she didn't like him. Or trust him. Maybe it was just the simple fact: Gabashvili had never known *him*. Not really, no matter what kind of vision he'd had. *He* belonged to her, to them, not to this stranger. But the way that he stood in front of the camera, his persona – it made the other two men shrink into the background. She'd begged Rob to wear a collared shirt, or at least trim his beard. He'd done neither. James was dressed in a similar suit as the newcomer, but he wore it like a used car salesman.

With everything set, Menendez flashed a smile at the men. Even Nykki was mesmerized. Whether it was sincere or not, that smile made her feel like she was the only person standing there.

"OK. Are we ready to get started?" she asked the men.

"Yes," Gabashvili responded with a smile. The other two muttered.

She explained how they would get B-roll of the activities underway and some footage of her explaining the history of the studio. But she wanted to do the interview first. The camera panned out to include all three of them. From off camera, Menendez lobbed the first softball question.

"What inspired you all to re-open this studio after the tragedy that occurred almost two years ago?"

Nykki smiled. There was something like closure to all of this, to getting to talk about their experiences, having them acknowledged. In a split second, she realized that the feeling was premature. James started to answer when Gabashvili talked over him:

"I became involved with this place because it was a way of adding back so much value to the community in the name of a man who had already given so much to it. It has been a real honor to be involved with the hardworking group of people who made all of this possible."

James glared at him the whole time, and as soon as the last syllable came out of his mouth he jumped in: "We wanted to honor my brother, our friend, by bringing back the place that he first created. I can't think of any better way of carrying on his name."

It carried on in this way for a painful fifteen minutes. Menendez would direct a question to one of the men and both of them would fight to answer. *What gave you the inspiration to do this*? And there they would go. *What was it like to have such a powerful experience*? Off they went. *How did all of you come together*? And so on and so forth until Nykki could barely stand to watch.

Through the whole time, Rob never looked up from the ground. He never uttered a single word for the interview. As it turned out later, they cut him out of the final tape for the broadcast, focusing just on the two alpha males battling to get their words in. Nykki endured the ordeal for him, though. And also, she finally admitted, to make sure that nothing truly tragic or misleading was said.

After the painful interview session was over, the camera crew headed inside. Some familiar and some new faces worked on incredible projects. Every medium was in use. A group of children received instruction in clay on the far side of the room. Others were discussing the painting classes with a group of visitors. The space was nearly overflowing with energy. Menendez directed the camera crew to the plaque by the inside of the door:

For the continuance of the social value and artistic energy
created by a dear friend and world-class artist.

James and Gabashvili had insisted on all the long, convoluted words. Nykki, Rob, and John had originally written just one line:

In loving memory of our dear friend.

In either case, she hoped, the loving memory was clearly communicated.

After what felt like an eternity of interrupting people for soundbites and snooping around the various corners of the place, the cameras were gone and the group finally had the chance to debrief together.

Never breaking character, Gabashvili smiled his TV smile. "I think that went very well. We should see some new business from that segment."

"Business?" Nykki asked him.

"You know what I mean."

"I'm not sure I do." She was embarrassed at her anger. More urgently, Rob was wide-eyed; she could see his skin almost crawling. Maybe the cameras had been more traumatic than she realized. He could have been a couple flashing lights away from an episode.

"There's no point in having this place open if no one comes," James answered.

"This place?" she snapped.

Rob turned suddenly and without a word slammed open the door and stepped outside.

"What's his problem?" James asked.

"He's naturally an introvert," Gabashvili mused.

"How would you know anything about him?" Nykki demanded. Fortunately, perhaps, his phone began to ring.

"Excuse me."

Nykki and James stood facing each other. He felt even more like a stranger to her in the suit.

"How did I do?" he asked.

She shrugged. *Who the fuck cares?* she wanted to ask. "Fine. I'm going to go check on Rob."

He shook his head. "You've always made your priorities clear. I guess he's next in line now?"

Without a conscious thought, she wheeled around and slapped him in the face. "You shut your goddamn mouth," she growled, shaking, almost inaudible. She turned back around and walked briskly outside. Rob was around the side, in the alley, squatting down and smoking.

He looked up at her from underneath the wild beard and untrimmed eyebrows. "Sorry."

"You don't have anything to be sorry for." She sat down beside him and took the cigarette from him.

"Come on. You worked really hard to quit," he said.

She shook her head. "I don't care." She burned almost all the rest of it in a single draw. He lit up two more.

"The cameras got to you, didn't they?" she asked.

He nodded, his eyes looking far away into some invisible place. "Yep." And all the fighting too, she knew.

She rubbed her hands over her face. "It was so...so painful."

"What did we do?" Rob asked. There was less panic, more desperation in his eyes.

"What do you mean?"

"Here. The studio."

She looked around, took a drag, then a deep breath. Stalling. "I don't know."

"I'm starting a new after-school program in a few weeks. I'll be doing it on their campus. Taking some of my woodworking gear down there."

"That'll be great," she said. But they'd known each other too long to carry on like that. "Have you been happy at all during this?"

"I was happy honoring *him*. I would do anything for *him*. And for you."

"You don't have to do anything for me," she said. "You don't owe me anything. I want you to do what's best for you."

"Taking care of you and taking care of this place is the only thing I can do to try to make things right. So that's what I'm going to do. No matter what."

She sat as he did, resolute. She studied his round, hairy face. She knew the look. He would do what he said, no matter what it cost.

Looking at Rob, now, was like the mirror of looking at *him*. Whatever she had seen, the man on the street and the other in the studio -- when this all began, those two men were like the same spirit in different forms. But Rob was the opposite now. He was a different spirit, different than he'd been even the months ago when she'd knocked on his door, but still in the same body. He looked the same, talked the same, but every day he disappeared a little more. A different spirit in the same form, bent over by the weight of his choices.

"What you owe is to live your own life. You don't have to live somebody else's life."

He nodded. But he was already gone. Still sitting there, still smoking. But gone.

John

John sat and fidgeted, reluctantly, in the stagnant, mold-scented dining room. He wasn't the coolest guy on Earth, he knew, but this place was really not his idea of a good time. Ceramic figurines of all shapes and sizes surrounded him on a variety of hutches, tables, and shelves. The beige carpet and overpowering air freshener transported him back to childhood at his grandmother's place. This was probably the most out of touch place possible for the leather jacket he was wearing. The old-time Wurlitzer electric organ sat unused, unplugged, but not touched by an ounce of dust.

Yet he was neither angry nor agitated about waiting a seeming eternity for her to leave the restroom and finally greet him. Her day nurse, Angelica, had been kind enough to let him in. The two had a long-standing appointment on this day and time, but gastric distress among the elderly was no respecter of social obligations. John knew, oh how he knew; he had done his time as a nursing home aide to pay for art school. He had changed diapers and bedpans and been the only person in the room when one of the residents gave up the ghost in the late hours of the night.

Maybe that really was why he was here in the first place. Nothing about trust or family; just a practical decision. *He* knew that John was capable of taking care of her in a way that no one else could, should the need arise. Skill-wise, a trained caretaker; temperament-wise, a balanced option between James' cold indifference and Rob's soft-hearted neuroticism that could lead to him being trapped here for days, eating an endless series of cookies, teas and meals.

Making sure that John would be there, at this place, had been *his* last words. It was the same as that night in the nursing home. The desperate look in the eyes and just that one request to take care of her. The complete refusal to attach any emotion to the memory, the only way that John knew how to hold it steady inside. He'd tried to bring it up with Nykki a couple times, early on, just to make sure that he hadn't imagined it. It was pointless; she was so ecstatic with grief that she didn't even remember John being there in the last moments.

If he were being honest, the figurines and old carpet had never really bothered him. It was the new stuff that was getting to him. A glass hutch that once hosted china and other tchotchkes now held a lifetime of pictures, newspaper clippings, and memorial gifts of and for her first-born son. It seemed that every print version of that night's events had been scrupulously clipped and framed. Every gift that someone had sent or left at her door was preserved and piled onto the shelves until it seemed the tangled mess might fall to the ground.

It was hard enough for him to keep being drawn back to the past. There was something about people at this age; a point they reached where they realized the future was a lot shorter than the past. It didn't seem to be nostalgia, really. Maybe just acceptance that it was unlikely that many new memories would be created in the future, that the only path was to make the most of remembrance.

But this case was a little different. Today, he consciously felt the twinge of resentment at each of these pieces. Anyone else would come and see a loving mother holding on to her son. But he could see the rest of the story, the real-time flow before and after all those mementos. He knew that she had worked hard, almost constantly, to get her son to stop his work. He had seen the conversations of her begging him to do anything else, to stop associating with those "questionable" artist-types, to start thinking about having a family and a career.

He sat with hands folded in his lap, pondering all of this, when she finally wheeled the walker down the carpeted hallway and snuck up on him. A person wouldn't have thought she would needed a walker; she wasn't yet bent over or particularly slow. But such was arthritis and neuropathy. The joints weren't locked up yet; they just caused her excruciating pain to move.

"Hello, son," she said with a smile. She sat more briskly than one might expect from the walker. She had called him that ever since her own son had passed, even though John was no blood relation.

"Hi," he said with a smile in return.

"Did Angelica offer you a drink or some snacks already?"

"Yes. I'm fine."

She nodded. "So...what's been happening this week?"

"Just getting everything ready for the move. Finally ready to go, I guess."

She chuckled a little. "You don't sound too convinced."

He looked down at the table. "It's just a big move. Never really thought about moving out of here. But I know it's the right thing."

"That's what really matters," she said. "As long as you do something because you really believe it to be right."

He nodded. He wasn't really sure about that part. He was much more clear about what couldn't be done and who it couldn't be done with. As to the details – he was too filled with excitement and anxiety to know if it was "the right" thing. All he knew, for sure, was that "the East" was a place he had never been – a place in the glorious undefined; a place full of people and excitement. All he felt was that possibilities existed, in that unknown place and that wonderful time known as the Future.

"How are you?" *Will you be OK without me?* That's the question he really needed answered. The one thing that really held him back.

There was no way to hide anything from her. "I'm going to be fine. I have Angelica, and James and Judith."

John knew what her own son had known. She would see Angelica a lot more than she would see James. He was afraid to think honest thoughts about James for fear that she would see them.

Judith visited a fair bit but had enough of her own issues to work through. She still needed a mother. John was unlucky enough to be there for a few of those visits. The poor old woman, who had lost so much, somehow had to muster strength to help and support a daughter that, by comparison, had been given almost everything. Of course, she had lost her brother – that was no small thing – but she'd grown up in a good home, with two biological, loving parents. Her father hadn't passed away until she was already grown and away at college. She'd never experienced the resentment of being some other man's child. Not that her brother had ever talked about it, but it was always there in his eyes and his art.

"Well, that's good." It was the best he could do. Not that he could ever really keep her from seeing his feelings. He knew her almost as well as he knew his own mother.

"So what are you actually going to be doing once you get out there?"

He was surprised. She seemed genuinely happy for him. He'd been so worried that she would be upset.

"I've already got some space rented and a few students I connected with online. So I'll be opening my own studio and teaching pretty much as soon as I get out there."

"You're going to do so well. I know your mother is so proud of you."

"Thank you." He couldn't help blushing a little.

"I appreciate you stopping by to see an old woman one more time, but it sounds like you have plenty to do without me taking up all of your time."

He shook his head; he was almost uncomfortable, defensive at the idea that he didn't want to be there. "No, no. It's fine. I'll call you every week. And if you ever decide you want to come with me there's always space for you."

He'd offered to let her move with him at least a hundred times. But each time he said it he never expected a yes. Nor did he receive one this time.

"It's time for you to go on and live your life, John. You don't always have to be worrying about other people."

"It's not a problem to worry about you."

"You have a good heart, but sooner or later you're going to have to worry about yourself a little bit."

The words sounded strange to him. He'd never held himself back from doing anything he wanted. He'd gone to the best art school that he could, moved hundreds of miles from his family. He'd been supported by friends and family in everything he'd wanted to do. And he had the greatest allies of all. Time. Youth. He lived almost unconsciously with these allies, relentlessly focused on all the bright possibilities of the future. Staring at the china hutch was what always brought it consciously to mind. The shocking difference of living with a face turned toward the past. Even before the hutch, she'd always kept a drawer full of postcards, regaling visitors with the tales of other peoples' journeys.

"I do want to ask you one thing before you go." Her demeanor was now markedly different, as though she'd just been kicked by a horse. It was enough to make John tense as well.

"Of course. Anything."

"What was it like? When you saw him?"

Somehow they'd never talked about this. He knew that it would surely happen one day, but how disappointing, he thought, that it had to be this day. It was something he'd spent a lot of time trying to figure out for himself. It was strange to him how something so real could be so hard to describe.

"It was like bathing in love. It was like freezing and then being set out to be warmed in the sun."

Even with this little bit of description – the abstract words that came easier to him than sights and smells – tears were already in her eyes.

She cleared her throat. "Was it him? Was it really him?"

He'd loved studying philosophy in school and loved nothing more than spending hours debating the meaning of *real*. But the school of hard knocks had taught him that this was neither the time nor the place. Words were only the husk of her deeper meaning. He would not mix words with her.

"Yes. There's no doubt in my mind. But you wouldn't recognize *him* with your eyes."

The dreaded moment – the first tear to fall. But she nodded, dutifully, like always.

"Maybe that's why he never came by to see me," she said, flat, exhausted.

"Maybe *he* did."

"I like to think I would've recognized him with my eyes. But you're right. I wouldn't be looking for him in some other way. I want to see him the way I remember him."

The words sounded brutal, but he knew what she meant. He knew that she would take any connection with him that she could get. But it was an honest longing for what she really wanted. He understood, if he were being honest. He'd felt it too, when the vision was first gone. Like your mother holding you when you were sick, and then leaving for the other room while you were still awake.

"I don't know if it would help," he said, "but maybe you'd like to see the studio? It might show you all the good that *he* did for other people?"

"The same studio that you're leaving?" she said with a sad lop-sided smile.

Really for the first time it dawned on him how unfair it was that he was the only one around to hear all this. Unfair to her, of course, but also to him. Why couldn't she tell James if she was unhappy with the way things were going? Or maybe she wasn't – maybe it was just her way of keeping her distance.

"No matter what happens at the studio, *he* did a lot of good for the cause that *he* cared about. He wanted to make a statement against injustice, and that's what he did. It led to changes well beyond what happened that night. He didn't just pursue art, he pursued art for the purpose of changing the world."

John had seen this before. A mother – or a father or a spouse – didn't want to hear about higher purposes. They only cared about the person. And when the person was gone, they were gone. In life's most wonderful and terrible moments, his mind went to all those higher, abstract places.

It took great effort and painful experience to understand that most people were dragged in those moments to their worst places. The presence of flesh and blood was no longer there to hold back the broken dam of guilt and remembrance. It made sense to him, consciously, of why some had seen the vision and then left the group. That kind of remembrance wasn't for everyone.

He knew it was time to go. He stood and hugged her. He knew it was for the last time. But he pressed ahead, to the Future, the infinite brightness of unrealized possibility.

Parousia

James had felt the urge to try a new coffeeshop that had just opened. It was a bit of hassle getting there since it was in the up and coming neighborhood on the other side of town. But he'd had the urge to try it because they were known for using only soy or coconut milk for their lattes. As he pulled around the corner, looking for a place to park near that shiny new hipster magnet, he saw an oddity as bold as life and unmistakable. Someone had painted an almost exact replica of Rob's mural, the one that he had painted on the wall of the old coffeeshop in the neighborhood where *he* used to live.

He had barely finished pulling over his car before he called Rob. It was well before noon, so Rob's voice was thick and gravelly when he answered.

"Somebody stole the mural," James shouted.

"What?"

"Rob, listen to me. Somebody copied your mural. The one that you painted down the street from the studio."

There was silence on the other end of the line. "OK," Rob finally muttered.

"I'm sorry," James snapped. "Are we not on the same page? Do you not see a problem with this?"

Another long pause. "Not really."

"You don't mind that somebody came along and just stole your copyright?"

"I don't...I don't give a shit about the copyright on that. That's not why I did it."

James scoffed. "Well, I have a major problem with it. You are a board member of the studio, so when somebody comes and steals your work, they're stealing from all of us. When they come and they take our message, then they're stealing our momentum and our resources."

"What?"

"What do you mean 'what'? Somebody is representing the people and the message of our studio. That is not OK."

"Well, what do you want to do?"

"What I *want* to do is have an immediate special board meeting and figure out how to respond to this. What I'm *going* to do right now is go into this place and find out who the hell did this."

"OK, well, let me know. I'll be there if there's a meeting."

James hung up abruptly and stormed into the shop. He cut around the line and shouted for a manager. He found nothing, and in his storm of rage left without even ordering the drink, swearing his eternal enmity for the establishment in the process. He channeled that fury into a barrage of phone calls, in which he managed to get the board assembled for the following night. He instructed everyone that he spoke with to spread the word that the meeting was open to the public in the hope of finding and shaming the person responsible for the public affront.

For his part, Rob arrived a couple minutes before the meeting was to start. It had taken him, like with most days, until mid-afternoon to get dressed and out the door. This gave him plenty of time to do one thing before the meeting. He called Nykki to find out exactly where James had seen the new mural. It was in a neighborhood where none of them had spent time in the past; very upscale, well on the path to being gentrified. It was easy to see the mural as he drove down the main road. It stood out, but was by no means the only mural to be found. This was the type of neighborhood where street art was friendly and commercial, not the work of vandals or protestors as might be the case elsewhere. The replica in question, though, was an exception; it stood apart as if Picasso had been painting in a high school art class.

He stood and marveled with the detached eye of the art critic. There were some strong similarities to his own work; it was an *almost* exact replica because the slight differences completely changed the aesthetics and the meaning of the final result. His own work, though displayed in public, was personal. Every stroke of the brush was filled with memory.

This new mural was different. It told the same story, but it was more impersonal; its point of focus was a bigger story, in which that hateful night was only a single manifestation. The chaotic mass of black and orange and white colors that Rob had used to paint *him* -- what one critic had called "a disturbing sign of deep trauma" – was reconstructed here with the faces of other victims from similar incidents of violence around the world. Up close, Rob could see only the faces. At a distance, they together reconstructed the same colors and shape that he himself had made.

Some of those faces were recognizable from high-profile media stories. Other faces were obscure; Rob found them later after extensive web searching, but even then they were names and faces that seemed to barely make the news in their own hometowns. All of which suggested an extensive process of research and thought. And then the seemingly impossible physical task of so quickly painting these tiny faces in excruciating detail.

He marveled at the exquisite work. He traced his hand over the faces he knew and those that he didn't. He stepped back again and wept at the sight of his friend, and then turned back to the business at hand.

After this detour, Rob stepped foot for the first time into the new board room of the studio. The group had taken out a lease on the floor above shortly after re-opening the studio. James and Gabashvili were insistent that they needed office space if they were to achieve their real potential. Still, after carving out room for a few offices, there was room for only twenty-two seats at the board table for the twenty-five board members. There were chairs for observers ringed around the back of the room. Those seats were filled with many current students of the studio and a few from other groups that sometimes visited. As a result, it was exceedingly cramped. Rob sat down between a few students he didn't know. He saw Nykki further down the row. She waved, but there were no seats beside her.

Just as James called the meeting to order, Thomas strolled in the door. He was dressed in wool slacks and a tee shirt, a tasteful choice displaying a kitten licking a rainbow-colored ice cream cone, plus a long wool knit robe that could easily be mistaken for a bathrobe. He stood for a moment, looking for a seat. There was a murmur; several of his university students were also students here, and they were excited to see him.

"What are you doing here?" James demanded.

Thomas shrugged. "The meeting is open to the public."

"It's open to people who care about our future and about the work we do here."

"I care about the work you do here," Thomas said. "I care about the recognition of the life spirit in the world around us."

James gave an exasperated shrug; there was really nothing he could say, as it had been his decision to open the meeting. Thomas walked toward Rob and put his hand on the young man sitting next to him.

"Hello, friend. The distinguished artist sitting next to you is a dear friend of mine, and I would be deeply appreciative if you would let me sit next to him."

The young man nodded, perhaps confused, and scurried across the room to find another seat. Thomas sat down next to Rob and patted his leg.

"Hello, friend," Thomas said.

"Hello, Professor."

"You still going to call me that after all these years? How much bullshit has James spoken so far?"

Rob inhaled deeply. There was the always-present residual cannabis smell that traveled with Thomas, but he seemed to be sober and relatively lucid at the moment. Not that he could be one to judge, he thought, having had a few pulls from his bourbon flask before coming in.

"Well, the meeting hasn't started yet."

Thomas laughed. James pounded the gavel.

"I want to thank everyone for gathering with us tonight. The size of this crowd is an obvious indicator of the importance of this issue and the opportunity that this presents for us to use this moment to clarify our purpose and direction.

"As certainly all of you know, I convened, as chair of the studio board, this special meeting as a chance to respond to a circumstance that has arisen. Recently, an unknown person or group replicated a mural known to be a representation of the founder of this studio. While it is not clear at this time what the purpose of this replication was, what we know for sure is that it will lead to confusion as to the proper use of the image of our founder and my brother."

There were a few random spots of applause in the room.

"Consequently, it is my proposal to this board that we make a formal statement on how and in what ways images of our founder can be appropriated. I have further proposed that this statement include a formal mission statement and, for the first time in our history, a formal statement of membership obligations and fees."

"Point of order," Thomas called.

"Points of order may only be called for by a member of the board," James replied.

"Point of order," Rob called.

"Yes?"

"I yield the floor to Thomas," he replied.

A few in the crowd snickered; others grunted.

Thomas stood and made another look around the room. "My point of order is to ask how your proposal is in any way connected to the painting of a mural."

"That's not a point of order."

Thomas sighed. "To put it in bureaucrat-speak, my point of order is that there is no basis of authority for the board to consider anything in your proposal."

James threw his gavel down onto the table. "Is this what you came to do, Thomas? To derail everything that we've tried to do over this last year?"

"I didn't join you before because I did not have the same visions that many of you had, nor would I have been compelled to this course of action by such a vision. Yet I never questioned the personal meaning of your visions to each of you. But the man who is gone was my friend too, and I will not stand by and have you desecrate **his** memory by turning **his** life's work into a soulless bureaucracy."

Gabashvili interjected with a mediator's tone. "Sir, all that the chairman is trying to say is that we have no idea who painted it, nor do we know how such images and messages could be further co-opted in the future. No one should be appropriating or monetizing his memory other than this official group."

"Sir? *Sir*?" Thomas snapped. "Do you not even know who I am?"

Gabashvili shook his head with a sincere look. "I'm sorry, I don't."

Thomas pointed at the bald Armenian. "That's understandable, because I don't even know who you are." There was a tense laugh around the room.

Thomas gave an exasperated smirk. "I'm serious. Who are you? Why are you sitting up there trying to run something? Rob should be sitting up there, not you."

There were a few cheers from somewhere in the room. Rob shook his head. "Don't do this," he whispered to Thomas.

Gabashvili gave a conciliatory nod. "Rob, would you like to trade seats with me?"

Rob shook his head. "Absolutely not."

Thomas continued, undeterred. "The man who brought us all together in the beginning would have had no use for formal statements and board meetings and membership fees or any other such pencil-pushing bullshit."

Judith interjected herself into the fight. She spoke with a slow, affected voice. Her brain had never fully recovered from the trauma of a car wreck years before. "If we can't have some rules, how are we supposed to make this place work? How are we supposed to make money to keep things going? Like the children's program and things like that?"

Thomas was gentler with her in his response. "You can have rules, and you can collect money. What you don't need is exclusion. No formal statements. No limits on the spirit of expression. No punishments for those who step outside the lines."

Thomas paused, and James jumped back in. "I spoke with the board and I know that we have a majority interested in making the aforementioned statements. The point of order is denied."

"That's like asking the fox how he feels about going into the henhouse," Thomas interrupted as he sat down. There was a hearty round of insults back from those at the table.

James carried on. "I have set the motion before you, with the text delivered to you prior to this meeting. Would any board member prefer to raise any points of discussion before we vote?"

Thomas swatted Rob's shoulder. "Come on. Say something."

Rob shrugged. "Like what?"

"Like how this is all a terrible idea."

Rob shrugged again. "I don't know if it is or not. I don't really care about any of this stuff."

"And so goes the most recent attempt to capture lightning in a bottle," Thomas mused to himself.

There were a few minutes of silence as everyone reviewed the pages one last time.

"Having had time to review these documents, I move that the board approve them as written," James said.

"Second," Gabashvili added.

"Any further discussion?" James asked.

"Now or never," Thomas whispered to Rob.

"Please state your agreement with an 'aye'," James said.

A clear majority stated their assent.

"And the 'nay's'."

There was silence. Some had clearly not voiced their opinion either way.

"The hottest place in hell, Rob," Thomas said with a smile.

Rob shook his head, looking away from his friend.

"The motion is approved," James said with a thump of the gavel. "I appreciate your attendance on such short notice. This special meeting is adjourned."

Nykki stood in front of Rob and Thomas as people began to mill about and leave.

"How did you vote?" Thomas asked.

She replied with silence.

"It is good to see you both. You're always welcome to stop by my home," Thomas said. He stood and gave them both a hug. "I won't even charge you any dues."

"It's good to see you, Thomas," Nykki said, hugging him for a couple extra seconds. "I know *he* would have been happy with what you said."

"I hope so. We all follow our vision where it leads. Don't let the past hold you so much that you lose sight of the future."

He turned toward the door when James suddenly appeared before him.

"Congratulations," Thomas said to him.

"Never come back here," James said.

"Even if I pay my dues?" Thomas asked with a smile.

"Never come back here," James said again.

Thomas nodded. "Don't worry. I won't." With that, he left the studio for the last time.

James turned his gaze toward Rob and Nykki. "The future is looking bright now."

"Is it?" she asked.

"I'm never going to be good enough for you, am I?"

Her face suddenly changed, as though something had broken. "This isn't about you. None of this is about you. But you don't get that."

"I'm just doing what has to be done. For everybody."

"No, you're doing what you want to do. For you."

James took a deep breath. "You shouldn't feel obligated to come back, either, if you don't want."

She nodded and moved for the door. Rob followed behind her.

"I'll keep that in mind. I will keep that in mind."

Missing

Nykki walked timidly into the space. She held the door so that it closed silently behind her, as though she were breaking and entering. It wouldn't have mattered if it had slammed shut. There were so many people, and so much noise, that no one would have really noticed anyway. The board had been discussing for some time the need for a larger space. The studio had become the epicenter of *avant garde* talent in the city. The demand was so great that there was now a full-time staff member to register visitors and manage the online calendar so that there could be as much access as possible. The old days of first-come, first-served were over.

She could see already that James was not in his office. It was hard to find him here during the day. He'd been asked to join the university as a professor emeritus or visiting professor or something like that. All she knew for sure was that he talked all the time about his class lectures. His connection there was only the beginning of a long onslaught from academia. It seemed like every day now that students and faculty from all of the area universities were coming to the studio. They studied *his* work scrupulously, seemingly mesmerized at being in the presence of paintings and 3D pieces that hung like sacred objects all around the studio. They stood in awe over Rob's magnificent red oak totem that was erected in the center of the studio space; they compared John's abstract paintings, which hung parallel with the ceiling, to Picasso and Pollock; they published in psychology journals about the meaning of James' savage color combinations. Quaint smiles always for Judith's small but expertly-crafted oil painting in the corner.

She walked through slowly, looking for any familiar faces. She knew Rob wouldn't be here. He was never here. The time that he spent connected with the studio was spent out in the neighborhood schools with his on-site art programs. He was still an emeritus member of the studio board but never attended.

Even Gabashvili was rarely seen these days. He had recently published a second book of visions, describing the mystical experiences he had had since becoming involved with the studio. He had never had those experiences in anyone else's presence, nor had he shared them while hanging around the place. He had another bestseller on his hands, so he would be traveling for at least a year on a book tour.

He was clearly not an artist. His work was the work of a mediocre high school student – proudly displayed because of a deep pride in the accomplishment, a childlike willingness to put it out to the world, and a lack of self-awareness for how much further he had to go to attain mastery. She did not think these things judgmentally; it was her detached artistic judgment. Perhaps others would judge it differently, as often happened in the artistic world.

Unlike the first, she had actually read his second book. There was no way that the man she had met and known for nearly a year could have been the one to write those pages. They spoke of feelings and emotions in a way that she had never seen from him. Never had there been a moment that was devoid of calculated self-interest. Everything he said was in service to some goal known only to him. To know him was to know a brand, not a man.

The one certain thing was the unbearable fighting between he and James. Every issue, no matter how small, had become an opportunity to test the loyalty of the group.

But this time she focused no longer on that world that had nothing to do with her. This one last time she let her mind free to see the ghosts in that place.

In that corner: a few artists from a local collective had painted together years earlier. She had bought from them a cityscape, now packed in the hatch of her Subaru.

That spot of paint on the floor: Judith coming to paint for the first time, so nervous and traumatized that she could barely hold the brush.

Enough was enough. More nostalgia would break her resolve. She laid a sealed letter on James' desk and moved briskly for the door.

She hoped her car would make it out of town, let alone all the way up the coast. Maybe it didn't really matter anyway. It was more of a vague feeling, a hunch, than a plan. There was no need to plan when there was no family to provide for, when no one would be expecting a call to let them know you made it safely. If the car died on the way up the coast she could always just say it was part of the plan all along.

In the city, sitting at a hundred red lights, there was nothing to do but smell exhaust and wonder how much longer the muffler could rattle until it fell off. She felt the pride of having worked a hundred night shifts, maybe more, to be able to save and buy this thing, though. So even if it was junk, it was her junk. They would be wondering where she was tonight, but even that didn't matter. Somebody went missing for a shift at least once a week. The manager would call a couple times, leave a hateful, profanity-laced message the second time, and then that would be it. She'd seen it plenty of times, so she knew the way out: she turned off her phone and threw it in the street as she turned onto the highway.

The letter to James was short, but it said all that needed to be said. She wouldn't be returning to the studio. It was time for her to seek a different path for herself. She couldn't be so bound to the past that she lost sight of the future.

After nearly an hour of battling through traffic, the city sounds were gone. It wasn't until trying to get out of the city that she could start to understand how much this place, this way of existence, was all-encompassing. Pressing out through the roads, the smells, the heat, the construction – it was like the levels of Purgatory, making sure that you were ready and worthy of the paradise that lay ahead. Pressing through this sheltered frame of existence must be a real choice. There would be no stumbling into the country, no leisurely Sunday afternoon drive. Leaving was a life choice, an existential decision – even if you chose to come back, which she didn't.

The arid mountains and the costal views were like a violent slap of paint into the senses. The real blue of the ocean was a jarring reminder that all the replicas of blue seen in the city were just a pale imitation. Even just driving beside the ocean was enough for her to feel the vastness of all the miles that lay on the other side of that sliver of coastline.

She imagined that the ocean water was drinking her; she was swimming in it and it absorbed her essence. The blanket of life's origin wrapped her up completely in this dream. She would have been happy, in that moment, to have it consume her and let her own consciousness come to a merciful end. Not to die, but to merge and become greater; to become part of that ever-moving life force that constantly changed the cosmos and pushed existence toward its final end. Or maybe toward the next cycle of rebirth. The waves and the sweetness of the salt water were like the life force in material form. The ebb and flow of their movement spoke all that needed to be known of the underlying force of nature.

But here she was, still encased in flesh, starting to think again of all the things she should be worried about. Where to live. What job to get. Where she was going to stay tonight. She used to have some family up this way, in the coastal area about six hours from where she was headed. But they were either dead now or had disowned her.

In her mind, it was for the best. This wasn't to reconnect. It was to get away. Further up the road, another hour or so, she saw a place to pull over, a small beach. It was a place she had gone as a child. She could still remember everything about that trip, in a good way.

The sand between her toes was warm and charged her with energy. Her smile was automatic and from deep in the heart. She had no swimsuit and there were too many people on this perfect day to find a private place to be naked. So she found a mound of sand to sit on where her toes could feel the water at the highest point of the tide. It was good enough. Good enough to melt the rest of the world away, completely. She closed her eyes and raised her chin to the sun in an act of thankful worship.

Then she opened her eyes and saw someone staring. Through the solar glare she could see this person's dark skin; the swagger of her hips; and most of all the fire in her eyes that struck her in an all-too-familiar way. She caught her breath, caught herself to make sure she didn't fall from her perch. She stared back without realizing it.

The woman stepped out of the glare and took a couple steps toward Nykki. Her dreadlocked hair washed over her shoulders, and she smiled.

"Hello," she said with a voice like a waterfall.

"Hi," Nykki said timidly.

The woman stopped, still looked at her.

"What's on your mind?" the woman asked.

Nykki shook her head. Could it really be?

"I don't understand," Nykki said.

The woman smiled still but raised an eyebrow. She swung a straw bag like a pendulum with her hands. "What are you trying to understand?"

"I didn't think I'd ever see you again."

The woman cocked her head. "I had the same thought about you at first. But I don't think we've met, have we?"

She felt like everything was spinning. "I...I thought so. But maybe not. You haven't met me before?"

The woman was now visibly confused, but instead of retreating she walked closer and knelt down in the sand. She studied Nykki's features, her eyes wandering along Nykki's eyes and nose and cheeks; her heart raced as the woman twirled a lock of her golden hair, her fingers grazing Nykki's shoulder.

"No, I haven't met you before," the woman said in an almost-whisper. "But I'm glad I'm meeting you now."

Nykki smiled and furtively wiped away a tear. "I'm sorry for sounding crazy. Just...missing someone. Thought I was seeing them again."

The woman nodded and pulled a handkerchief from her bag. "I understand."

"Thank you."

"It's hard when someone is really gone," the woman said.

She nodded. "My name is Nykki."

"Sonya."

"That's a beautiful name."

Sonya moved to sit beside her on the sand hill, their hips lightly touching. She was dressed in a single piece bathing suit with a long wrap around her waist, covering her hips and thighs.

"Thank you. So is Nykki."

"Am I keeping you?" Nykki asked.

"No. I'm here by myself, just getting a little sun while I do some reading."

They sat together quietly.

"Who did you lose?" Sonya asked.

Nykki sighed. "The love of my life."

"Me too."

"I thought I was seeing him. That's why I was acting so crazy."

Sonya looked her over again. "I thought you were her. You looked so much like her at a distance."

Nykki hated all the years in the city that made her so cynical. What a way of working your way into someone's confidence, to say something like that. You could say that to anyone, make them feel a connection to you. This was the perfect time for Sonya – or whoever she was – to find some way to take advantage of her.

Sonya pulled her wallet out of the bag. "Look," she said.

Nykki looked, and it was indeed shocking. Sonya and the blonde, Nordic woman kissing at a restaurant. Nykki looked at Sonya's lips just a few inches from hers; she leaned in to look at the stranger's photos. Maybe it was possible that she *had* kissed them before, or that she had some kind of connection to this person who had. The next photo: the two women at their wedding. Both smiling.

"Cancer," Sonya said.

Nykki watched her thick, beautiful lips as she said the words. "What?"

"She died of cancer. Three years ago."

"I'm so sorry."

Sonya did not cry nor even make an expression. She just shook her head and let the constant drain of exhaustion slip to the surface. "The hardest part, once you get through grief, is the loneliness, and then the desperation of trying to find any meaning."

"I guess I'm just getting to that last part."

"What happened to your love?"

Nykki bowed her head into the handkerchief. "Murder."

"Oh my god...." Sonya put her arm around her. "Did they find who did it?"

"Oh yes. Their badge numbers were plain as day. He had been painting a mural. He was protesting someone else's murder. Ironic, I guess. They came to tell us all to leave and to make him stop painting and he wouldn't. Then after they killed him they spread all the lies about how he was a criminal, resisting arrest, trespassing. He didn't do any of those things. I was there. I saw everything that happened. The state said it was justified. They never took my witness statement."

"I'm so sorry," Sonya said. "Was this the incident downtown, a couple years ago?"

"Yes."

"Can I tell you something about that night?"

Nykki nodded.

"I was so disturbed by that story that I wanted to learn more about him. I was so inspired by what I read and by the mural he was working on that I made a painting in his honor."

Nykki looked at her, self-conscious of how red and swollen her eyes must be. "You're a painter?"

She nodded. "Yes, I teach painting at the college here. I enjoy teaching but I love painting. And sculpting."

"What kind of paint?"

"Mostly acrylic. But for your love I used oil."

"Oil was his favorite."

"Well," Sonya paused, "if you don't have anywhere to be, maybe I could show it to you. Then we could have dinner." Her voice trailed off timidly.

Nykki was stricken with panic. She *felt*. She hadn't felt anything but numbness and loneliness in forever; it felt so unsafe to feel anything else.

"I'm sorry. I hope I didn't make you uncomfortable," Sonya said.

"Oh, no. I'm sorry. Yes, I could have dinner."

Nykki drove close behind Sonya's red convertible about ten miles farther north. Nykki couldn't take her eyes off the scarf, tied around the cap of Sonya's straw hat, that danced around in the wind. It seemed like the kind of situation that she should be anxious about. But for some reason she wasn't. They pulled down a dirt road about a quarter mile, into the driveway of a rustic cabin. The homes on this road were small, but given the part of the state and how close they were to the ocean, these places cost a small fortune. Sonya's was a perfect bohemian place. Random pieces of handmade glassware decorated the yard. Blue and yellow paint fading on the wood siding and window trim. What seemed like handmade wind chimes. This was the home that Nykki had always dreamed of having.

"Home sweet home," Sonya called. Indeed, Nykki thought. Rather than going straight inside, Sonya walked back toward a newer metal building behind the house. It was almost as big, in fact, as the house itself. Dogs barked from inside.

"This is my studio back here," Sonya said as Nykki caught up with her. The door was unlocked. How unsafe, Nykki thought instinctively. The inside, though, was remarkable. Seventy-one degrees; she could feel it. The perfect temperature, with low humidity, for keeping art safe in a typical setting. The room was large enough for several easels, all of which had works in progress.

"Are those all yours?" Nykki asked.

"No. I have friends and students who come over to work here when the college gets too loud." Sonya touched the canvas closest to the door, a dark urban cityscape with a burst of light in the very middle of the frame. "This one is mine."

"It's incredible."

Nykki was genuinely amazed, but her eyes were drawn to the vast number of paintings on the walls. Some she recognized; lithographs and paintings from artists everyone would know. Others were on unframed canvases. She knew, right away, the one she'd been looking for.

"That's the one," Nykki said, unable to break her gaze.

"Do you like it?"

She couldn't speak; the sight of him jarred her too much. She cried into Sonya's shoulder. Sonya wrapped her up in a hug.

"I'm so sorry," Sonya said. "Maybe this wasn't a good idea."

"No. No. It's beautiful." She could feel what she wanted to say, but she couldn't say it. Sonya had given him to the world. The perfect image of him, spreading his hands in blessing over the city that had killed him; it was the image of him that Nykki thought only she could see – the perfection of love, the healing of his mercy; a god of light and sorrow, barely contained in flesh. A man made victorious, not defeated, by death.

The source of the singular, stabbing pain was clear: he didn't belong only to her anymore. He belonged to the world now; the secret vision of his love, the love she always wanted to be just for her, was now for everyone.

"How long did it take?" Nykki asked when she could finally speak.

"Weeks. But he's worth it, isn't he?"

Sonya held her as she was slowly able to turn her face back toward the painting.

"So many things I still want to say," Nykki whispered.

"There's time. Say them when you're ready."

There was no point. The things she would say would just be trophies for Death – proof of all the things Death had taken by taking him away.

"We'll come back here. Let me make you dinner, and you can rest and come back here when you're ready."

It was a dinner fit for the coast – salmon and tomatoes, all with rosemary and kale. Nykki slept while Sonya cooked. It was at first a vigilant watch from the couch, which turned into a hard sleep curled up. The first deep sleep she had had in years. Sonya's touch waking her from sleep was as heavenly as the cooked rosemary. They ate in the familiar silence that soldiers and old friends share. The sun cast a shimmer into the room as it began to set on the horizon.

"You need a place to stay?" Sonya asked. Part question and part statement.

"No. I'll figure something out."

"You should stay here tonight. Just to rest," Sonya said. "I will take the couch. You can have my bed. It's a perfect bed," she said with a cheeky, self-indulgent smile.

"No. I can't trouble you."

"You're no trouble at all," Sonya said, clearing her plates. Accepting generosity was the hardest thing of all.

"What do you want from me?" Nykki asked. The years of fear and mistrust could be contained no longer. She didn't want to hurt Sonya, but she did. It was the only way to get back to the safe place, the place of no-feeling.

Sonya sat down in a chair at the corner of the table. She looked intently into Nykki's eyes.

"This is all an elaborate plan to kidnap you," she said, her face stone cold. Then they both broke into laughter. Then they kissed. Pressing into each other, hands reaching to find what they felt in their memories, tongues swirling around each other's mouths. Then they hit those memories and pulled away, as quickly as they had come together.

"I wanted *that*. I want to feel the life and the love that I have to believe is still in the world," Sonya said.

I don't want to betray him, Nykki thought. But when she thought the words, all she could see was the painting. He was no longer hers. Not gone, but not hers.

"I want that, too," Nykki whispered. Everything in Sonya's voice and warmth and words felt so familiar.

"There's time. You don't have to feel it all at once. But you should stay here, in my home, tonight. Let me take care of you."

Nykki acquiesced. It had been so long since she had been taken care of. Not since that night when he brought her in from the cold, from the dark aloneness, into his loving shelter. Now there was that same feeling as she slipped into the silk sheets on the bed. As she called to Sonya just as her host was going into the next room. As they embraced each other and tangled up in the sheets. As they knew that neither was ready for more, at long last, than a true night's rest. As they slept, together, at peace with that part of themselves that had been missing.

Made in the USA
Middletown, DE
06 January 2020

82630334R00059